The Legend of Sleepy Hollow

Library of Congress Cataloging-in-Publication Data

Hitchner, Earle.
    Legend of Sleepy Hollow / by Washington Irving; retold by Earle
Hitchner; illustrated by John Van Buuren.
        p.   cm. (Troll illustrated classics)
        Summary: A superstitious schoolmaster, in love with a wealthy
farmer's daughter, has a terrifying encounter with a headless
horseman.
        ISBN 0-8167-1869-5 (lib. bdg.)   ISBN 0-8167-7238-X (pbk.)
        [1. Ghosts—Fiction.   2. New York (State)—Fiction.]   I. Van
Buuren, John, ill.   II. Irving, Washington, 1783-1859.   Legend of
Sleepy Hollow.   III. Title.
PZ7.H6296Le   1990
[Fic]—dc20   89-33942

This edition published in 2002.

The Legend of Sleepy Hollow

WASHINGTON IRVING

**Retold by
Earle Hitchner**

**Illustrated by
John Van Buuren**

Troll

Many strange stories were told about the Hudson River valley known as Sleepy Hollow. Some people said it was bewitched. Others said an ancient Indian chief had cast a spell over it. There was talk of ghosts, goblins, haunted houses, and eerie phantoms at night.

But of all these stories, none struck greater terror into the hearts of the people than that of a figure on horseback without a head. This was the Headless Horseman! According to the villagers, he had fought for the British during the Revolutionary War. One day in battle, a rebel cannonball whistled toward him. Before the horseman could bat an eye, the cannonball had sheared his head off. It was never found. And the horseman was buried headless in the churchyard of Sleepy Hollow.

But the Headless Horseman does not lie buried there peacefully. Every night, he rises from his grave, mounts his horse, and gallops off in search of his head. He searches and searches until just before daybreak. Then, like a blast of wind, he returns to the churchyard and his grave before the morning sun can reach him.

Many of the villagers claim they've seen the Headless Horseman dashing across the valley late at night. He's a towering man cloaked in black, they say, and he rides a fierce black horse. Only a fool would cross his path during one of his midnight romps.

Ichabod Crane, Sleepy Hollow's schoolmaster, shared the villagers' opinion of the Headless Horseman. Ichabod wanted nothing to do with such a fearsome creature, though he loved to hear stories about him. The schoolmaster enjoyed all kinds of ghost and goblin stories. When class ended in the afternoon, he'd often leave the one-room schoolhouse and lie under a tree. There, resting on soft grass, he'd spend hours reading books about witches and spirits and sorcerers.

In school, however, Ichabod Crane was not the dreamy person he was outside it. He insisted on strict obedience and attention from his pupils. If students really tried but failed, he'd correct them lightly. But if the school's bullies gave him trouble, he'd take a long birch rod and use it on them.

These whippings were not as bad as they could have been. For Ichabod Crane was by no means a strong or stout man. In fact, he looked very much like his last name. Behind his back, the schoolchildren giggled at the sight of their teacher walking along. His clothes fluttered in the breeze. He looked like a scarecrow let loose from the cornfield.

Outside the schoolhouse, Ichabod ignored the snickering of his pupils. He knew he'd have to stay in their good graces if he hoped to stay at their parents' houses. It was the custom then for parents to give the local schoolmaster food and lodging under their own roofs. Usually this lasted a week. Then the schoolmaster would move on to another house for the following week.

While staying at these houses, Ichabod tried to be useful. He helped pitch hay, mend fences, take the horses to water, drive the cows from pasture, and cut firewood. He also played with the younger children and even rocked the babies' cradles. And to make extra money, he gave singing lessons to the children and sometimes to their parents.

But in return, Ichabod expected more than just a plain bed and plain food. He liked being pampered. And despite his frail frame, he was a big eater. He loved creamy puddings and fresh-baked pies, plump turkeys and tender beef, and cakes and tarts with thick, sweet icing. All of this food was usually prepared for him by the mother and daughters of the household. And if a daughter was pretty, Ichabod would do his best to get in her good favor.

The schoolmaster already had one advantage in that he was well respected for his learning. In fact, only the local minister was considered superior in knowledge. Much to the envy of the local young men, Ichabod would use his education to impress the women. He'd recite poetry for them and read for their amusement the words chiseled on the churchyard tombstones. He'd also pass along gossip he managed to overhear at the houses he lodged at.

Ichabod's imagination, however, would often get away from him. Right up until dark, he'd read the stories about ghosts and witches he loved so much. Then, in the gathering gloom of night, he'd start back to the house he was staying at. Around him frogs croaked, screech owls hooted, and trees sighed. To Ichabod, these were the sounds of supernatural creatures moving in the dark. He'd walk along nervously, whistling or humming a tune as he went, his eyes darting from side to side.

Once, as he hurried along, Ichabod saw several very bright lights whizzing through the air around him. He immediately covered his face in terror, thinking they were spirits. But a buzzing noise made him peer through his hands. He realized that the lights were simply fireflies flitting through the darkness.

Relieved, Ichabod moved along. But he'd taken only a few short steps when a large, black beetle whizzed past his head. At that, Ichabod broke into a run. And he ran all the way back to where he was staying that night, convinced that the beetle was a witch transformed, hot on his heels.

Once inside the safety of the house, Ichabod would act as if nothing had happened. He'd slide his chair closer to the fire, where a row of apples was roasting and spluttering along the hearth. Then, he'd once again tell his tales of ghosts and goblins to the endless fascination of his hosts. They, in turn, would tell him their own stories of haunted fields, bridges, brooks, barns, and houses. And always the talk would turn back to the Headless Horseman, that galloping night rider feared by all the people of Sleepy Hollow.

Of all the houses Ichabod Crane lodged at, the one he looked forward to visiting the most was the Van Tassels'. The owner, Baltus Van Tassel, was a very wealthy man. He had a vast farm nestled in a green, fertile area along the banks of the Hudson River. A great elm tree spread its branches at the foot of the farm. An immense barn housed livestock and the harvest. Baltus Van Tassel owned the finest cattle, chickens, pigs, ducks, geese, and mules in the entire valley. His meadows were densely planted with wheat, rye, and corn. His orchards were full of trees and shrubs bearing luscious apples, grapes, berries, and melons.

The house he lived in with his wife and daughter was even more impressive than his surrounding lands. Spacious, with more rooms than Ichabod could count, it contained hand-crafted furniture of delicate beauty. There were also the basics of farm life—butter churns, leather saddles, harnesses, spinning wheels, and copper pots and kettles.

Every time Ichabod entered the Van Tassel estate, he dreamed of how it would feel to be its lord and master. He couldn't look at a pig without seeing a baked apple in its mouth. He pictured the ducks swimming not in water but in thick, brown gravy. Ichabod also thought of the enormous amount of money he could get by selling off sections of the Van Tassel property. And he dreamed of the sleek thoroughbred horse he'd buy for himself with his wealth.

To win the house, barn, land, and holdings eventually, Ichabod knew he'd have to win the hand of the owner's only child, Katrina, in marriage. What made this prospect especially inviting was the extraordinary beauty of Katrina. A blooming girl of eighteen, she had a peach complexion, rosy cheeks, sparkling blue eyes, and golden-blond hair. The lads would practically fall over themselves when she went into town to shop. Katrina made them timid when near and heartsick when afar. She had stolen the heart of every single young man in Sleepy Hollow.

Ichabod was no exception. He used every opportunity when visiting the Van Tassels to sit next to Katrina. He told her funny stories, tried to impress her with his knowledge, and praised her beauty. He'd even sing for her or whistle a tune. Ichabod was determined to win her favor and, hopefully, her hand in marriage. He'd think of what his life would be like with her. It would be one of ease and comfort and riches. He would no longer have to teach unruly, thick-headed students. He would no longer have to depend on the kindness of their parents for a meal or a bed. He'd live a life of luxury—the life he believed he was entitled to.

The one major rival Ichabod had for Katrina's affection was a broad-shouldered lad named Brom Bones. He had thick, wavy black hair and a handsome, rugged face hinting at mischief. Far and away, Brom Bones was the strongest and boldest of all the young men in Sleepy Hollow. He was famed for his horsemanship. Riding his fiery steed, Daredevil, Brom never lost a race and few dared challenge him to one. Together, Brom and Daredevil would race across the countryside at night. Brom would whoop and holler as he rode, and Daredevil's sweat-flecked legs would gleam in the moonlight.

Brom Bones was also a ferocious fighter, ever ready for a scrap at the slightest challenge. He had defeated the toughest, meanest men in the valley. And his word had the force of law. Disputes were settled and scuffles stopped as soon as he stepped between people. Brom had a devilish sense of humor, too. He enjoyed practical jokes and outrageous pranks. Anything for a good laugh—that was Brom Bones' way. Whenever word came that a madcap stunt or fierce brawl had occurred nearby, the neighbors would shake their heads and say, ''Brom Bones again!'' They looked on him with grudging admiration.

For some time now, Brom Bones had singled out Katrina Van Tassel as his future bride. And it was whispered among the villagers that Katrina did not reject his advances. When the valley's young men learned of Bones' intentions toward Katrina, they quickly bowed out of the picture. All, that is, except Ichabod Crane.

Brom Bones resented Ichabod. He did not like the schoolmaster lingering around the Van Tassel farm. And he especially hated to see Ichabod in the company of Katrina. Every chance he got, Brom and his rowdy friends would make fun of Ichabod. But the schoolmaster ignored them, just as he ignored his pupils outside of class. Ichabod was careful to avoid any direct meeting with Brom. He did not want to give Brom any opportunity to pick a fight with him. So the schoolmaster turned a deaf ear to the insults Brom hurled at him in town. And he continued seeing Katrina.

Bones seethed with rage. He boasted that he would "double up the schoolmaster and lay him on a shelf in his own schoolhouse." Try as he did, though, Brom could not provoke Ichabod into fighting him. Every failure inflamed Brom's desire to make Ichabod's life miserable. With his gang of roaring comrades, Brom smoked out the schoolhouse by stopping up the chimney. Another time, he broke into the one-room building and turned all the desks and chairs topsy-turvy.

But Brom didn't stop there. He taught his dog to whine in a voice remarkably like Ichabod's singing voice. Brom would use the flimsiest excuse to go over to the Van Tassel farm when Ichabod was visiting and make fun of him. He even brought along the dog. It would whine on cue as Ichabod sang in the Van Tassel parlor.

This abuse continued for weeks. Brom got angrier and angrier as Ichabod spent more and more time with Katrina. Everyone in the village wondered when—and how—the feud would end.

One bright fall afternoon, the situation began to change, though no one knew it at the time. Ichabod was teaching his students in the schoolhouse. They were particularly quiet and attentive that day. In his hand, Ichabod held a short ruler. He had just used it on an unruly pupil. On the desk in front of the schoolmaster were items he had collected from the students: half-munched apples, pea shooters, popguns, paper animals, and spitballs. Hanging on the wall behind him was the dreaded birch rod.

As his pupils bent over their books, reading intently or trying to look as if they were, a horse galloped right up to the schoolhouse steps. Then came raps on the door. Ichabod said, "Enter," and in walked a servant holding a note. He gave it to Ichabod and then, with a curt nod of his head, left.

Ichabod told his students to keep their eyes on their books, not on him. Once more, the children buried themselves in their reading. As they did, Ichabod silently opened the note and read it. YOU ARE CORDIALLY INVITED TO A PARTY AT THE VAN TASSEL ESTATE TONIGHT. RESPECTFULLY, BALTUS VAN TASSEL. Ichabod's eyes bulged as he reread the invitation. A party! Where Katrina would be! And food, glorious food!

Ichabod slipped the note into his pocket. Then he whisked his students through the rest of their lessons. The pupils didn't know why they had to hurry through their school-work. Nor did they really care. All they knew was that Ichabod Crane dismissed them one hour earlier than normal. Suddenly set free, they burst through the open door of the schoolhouse and raced home.

Ichabod wanted to use the extra hour to freshen up and dress himself properly for the party. Using a broken mirror in the schoolhouse, he shaved and washed his face. He combed and recombed his hair. Then he took down his best suit from the side of the blackboard. It was rusty black. He brushed it and then put it on carefully. Ichabod smiled at himself in the mirror. Katrina couldn't help but be impressed, he thought.

Ichabod wanted to make sure his arrival at the Van Tassels' farm was just as impressive. So he borrowed a horse from the farmer he was staying with. Gunpowder was the horse's name. He was a gaunt, shaggy, broken-down old plow horse. He had a tail knotted with burrs, a neck like a turkey's, and a head like a hammer. One of his eyes was bad, giving the animal an odd, glassy stare.

Gunpowder's short stirrups made Ichabod's bony knees ride high in the saddle. His sharp elbows stuck out like a grasshopper's legs. As Gunpowder trotted along, Ichabod's arms flapped up and down like the wings of some gawky bird. His black coat fluttered behind him like a sail. And a small wool hat rested half on his forehead, half on his nose.

This comical sight proceeded through the countryside at a lazy pace. As he rode along, Ichabod came to orchards in the process of being harvested. Ripe, red apples hung heavy on the branches. Others had already been picked and put into baskets below. Still others had been heaped together, ready to be squeezed into cider.

Farther on were great fields of Indian corn. Many of the stalks had been stripped of their ears. Empty husks and chaff lay on the ground around them. And scattered among the stalks were big orange pumpkins, with their round bellies turned upward to the sun.

All seemed right with the world as Ichabod gently guided Gunpowder along the country lanes. There was a fresh, sweet scent in the air. Ichabod breathed in deeply. He was happy. He was going to see his beloved Katrina and to savor the wonderful food her family always served on these special occasions. Thoughts of Brom Bones and his bullying friends were far behind him. Ichabod started to whistle.

Soon the sun dropped in the west. Just ahead, Ichabod could see the Van Tassel estate. He rode Gunpowder right up to the rail where all the other horses and carriages had been tied. Among them was Daredevil. But Ichabod didn't notice him as he quickly tied Gunpowder to the rail and hastened inside.

The house was overflowing with people dressed in their finest clothes. The men wore polished leather boots, shiny pewter buckles, and pressed breeches and coats. The women wore starched, long-waisted gowns, prim petticoats, and close-crimped caps. The smell of powder and perfume and rouge filled the air. There was a joyful, giddy atmosphere in the Van Tassel home this evening. Everyone was having a marvelous time.

Moving through the throng of guests, Ichabod followed his nose to the food. On linen-covered tables were large silver platters heaped with the choicest foods. Ham, smoked beef, broiled salmon, roasted turkeys and chickens, candied ducks, and pheasant meat were on one table. On another were crullers, sweet cakes, shortcakes, ginger cakes, honey cakes, apple pies, peach pies, pumpkin pies, plum and peach and pear preserves, and rice and bread puddings. And a shorter table had bowls of cream and milk on it as well as tea and cider.

27

Baltus Van Tassel greeted Ichabod. With a leg of turkey still in his mouth, Ichabod mumbled hello. Then Baltus moved off into the crowd. He shook hands, slapped shoulders, and invited one and all to help themselves.

Ichabod was eating a slice of ham when the sound of music came from the large hall in the house. He drew closer to the hall and saw a fiddler nimbly moving his bow across the strings of his fiddle. On the dance floor, couples swirled together, keeping time to the music. Putting down his supper plate, Ichabod went over to Katrina and asked her to dance. She accepted, and soon the two were gliding over the floor together. Standing off against a wall was Brom Bones. He glared at Ichabod dancing with Katrina.

When the music stopped, Ichabod bowed to Katrina and asked her to save him the next dance. Then Ichabod headed to the pastry table and took a cruller. Nibbling it, he walked over to where a group of men were engaged in a spirited conversation. They were talking about the Revolutionary War and their own roles in it.

These war stories soon yielded to ghost stories. Ichabod was delighted. He listened to tales of funeral trains and of a woman in white who haunted Raven Rock. The schoolmaster also heard the story about an army major captured in the war whose wailings could still be heard near the tree where he was seized. Then, as always, the subject of the Headless Horseman came up.

"I hear he's been patrolling the woods again," said one man.

"With my own eyes," said another man, "I've seen his horse among the graves in the churchyard."

"Remember what happened to old Brouwer?" piped up a third speaker. "He met up with the Headless Horseman late one night by the bridge near the church. Off they galloped, neck and neck, until the horseman changed into a skeleton and threw old Brouwer headfirst into the brook."

All the men nodded their heads. What had happened to old Brouwer was common knowledge. It was also well known that the Headless Horseman would not cross over the bridge. Once on the other side, a person would be safe from him.

"I beat the Headless Horseman at his own game!"

The men stopped talking and looked at the person who spoke so brashly. It was Brom Bones.

"Well, I *would* have beaten him," said Brom, "if he'd played fair. I was riding in the valley one night when Daredevil and I came across him. Then and there, I challenged him to a race. The winner would get a bowl of punch. So off we went, blazing down the path along the brook. Daredevil beat the goblin horse, all right. But just as we got to the bridge, the horseman bolted over the churchyard wall and vanished in a flash of fire."

All these stories made a deep impression on Ichabod. And he told some of his own, recalled from the many afternoons he spent reading on the grass. Tale after tale was told. Little attention was paid to the music just started up again in the hall.

As the tales were spun, some of the men took out their pocket watches. None of them wanted to be out on the open roads at midnight. That was the time when the Headless Horseman was known to roam the countryside. The women were also getting fidgety about the lateness of the hour. No one was out on the dance floor.

The fiddler put away his fiddle, husbands and wives got their coats and hats, and soon everyone was leaving. Baltus Van Tassel saw his guests off, bidding them a safe trip home. Carriages and horses started pulling away from the rail. Hands waved from down the lane. An inky darkness had now set in. Only a thin sliver of moon cast what little light there was.

Ichabod was the only guest remaining. The schoolmaster was determined to speak with Katrina privately. He thought he had the upper hand in his pursuit of Katrina. He sat closer and spoke softly to her. There was tenderness in his voice as he talked. But Katrina's face was blank. And when she leaned over at last and spoke to Ichabod, the color drained from his face. He had a sad, stricken look. Then, when she was finished, he jumped to his feet and looked for his hat and coat.

Whatever Katrina said to Ichabod was clearly not what he wanted to hear. Had she been misleading him all along? Did she secretly desire Brom Bones and use the schoolmaster to make him jealous? No one knew but Katrina herself. And she never told.

Ichabod couldn't get out of the Van Tassel home fast enough. He grabbed his coat and hat, bid Katrina good night, and left. Outside, he went straight to Gunpowder, the only horse still tied to the rail. Ichabod untied and mounted him. Then, with several hearty cuffs and kicks, he urged Gunpowder down the road.

Gunpowder did not like being treated so roughly by the schoolmaster. Every step of the way, the horse resisted Ichabod's efforts at speeding forward. He often veered to the side. Other times, he'd slow to barely a walk. And once, he stopped outright and munched on some roadside berries.

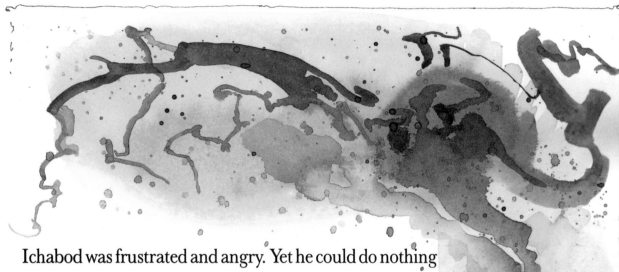

Ichabod was frustrated and angry. Yet he could do nothing with the horse. Gunpowder had a mind and will of his own.

It was now the very witching hour of night. Darkness engulfed Ichabod and Gunpowder. Pale moonlight glinted off the leaves of the trees. Their gnarled branches almost looked like arms reaching out to grab Ichabod. It must be close to midnight, he thought.

Sometimes in the dead hush, Ichabod could hear the distant barking of a watchdog. Now and then, he heard the faint cry of a faraway bird. And once in a while, a cricket chirped or a bullfrog bellowed from a nearby marsh.

The night grew darker and darker. The stars seemed to drop in the sky. Occasionally they were hidden by drifting clouds. Ichabod clutched the reins tightly around Gunpowder's neck. Surrounded by darkness, feeling cold in the hands and heart, he had never been so lonely. Hours earlier, he had traveled these same roads, happy. Now, he was traveling back utterly miserable.

What made his heart sink even lower was the sight of an enormous tree looming ahead in the middle of the road. Its limbs were twisted and huge. Some were as large as whole trees. This was where the army major had been captured. This was where his cries supposedly could still be heard. The people of Sleepy Hollow believed the tree was cursed and that strange beings lived among its branches.

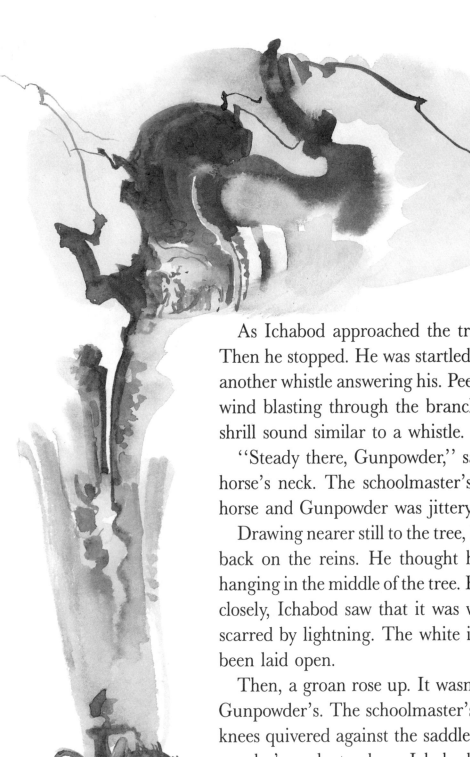

As Ichabod approached the tree, he began to whistle. Then he stopped. He was startled by what he thought was another whistle answering his. Peering up, he could see the wind blasting through the branches. This was making a shrill sound similar to a whistle.

''Steady there, Gunpowder,'' said Ichabod, patting the horse's neck. The schoolmaster's fear had spread to the horse and Gunpowder was jittery.

Drawing nearer still to the tree, Ichabod suddenly pulled back on the reins. He thought he saw something white hanging in the middle of the tree. But when he looked more closely, Ichabod saw that it was where the tree had been scarred by lightning. The white interior of the wood had been laid open.

Then, a groan rose up. It wasn't Ichabod's. Nor was it Gunpowder's. The schoolmaster's teeth chattered and his knees quivered against the saddle. Even the hair on Gunpowder's neck stood up. Ichabod heard the groan again. Craning his neck upward, the schoolmaster saw two large branches swaying in the breeze. They were rubbing against each other. The sound they made was that of wood groaning as it bent. Ichabod breathed easier. He passed by the tree safely.

About five hundred yards ahead of him was a brook running parallel to the road. Farther down was a bridge made of heavy planks. And on the same side of the road Ichabod was on, to the right of the bridge, was the churchyard of Sleepy Hollow.

To get across this bridge would be the toughest test of all, Ichabod knew. Both brook and bridge were considered haunted. Even during the day, in bright sunlight, local schoolchildren would walk a mile out of their way to avoid crossing it.

Ichabod looked from side to side, trying to see if anything or anyone was hidden there. He kept Gunpowder moving forward. Closer and closer he came to the brook. His heart was thumping loudly inside him. Then, when he could no longer stand the tension, Ichabod sharply kicked Gunpowder in hope of galloping quickly down and across the bridge. His heels dug into the flanks of the horse. He even added a few extra kicks for good measure. Ichabod desperately wanted to be over the bridge and safe.

But Gunpowder refused to cooperate. Instead, the horse bolted sideways into a thicket of brambles. By the time Ichabod reined the horse out of the thicket, he was covered with the prickly leaves. But he didn't care. He had to get across that bridge!

Once more, Ichabod kicked and reined Gunpowder sharply. He even used a short whip on the horse's ribs. Snuffling and snorting, Gunpowder gave in a little. He started to trot briskly ahead. But the horse was not moving anywhere near as fast as Ichabod wanted. The bridge was still at least two hundred yards away.

Suddenly, Gunpowder came to a dead halt. The force of it nearly pitched Ichabod over the horse's head. Enraged, the schoolmaster was about to whip the animal once more when a twig snapped behind him. Looking backward, Ichabod turned white as chalk. Even Gunpowder, angling his head around, had his ears pinned back in fright. Just a hundred yards behind Ichabod and his horse, something huge and misshapen lurked in the shadows. It didn't move— it seemed to be waiting for the horse and rider in front of it to make the first move.

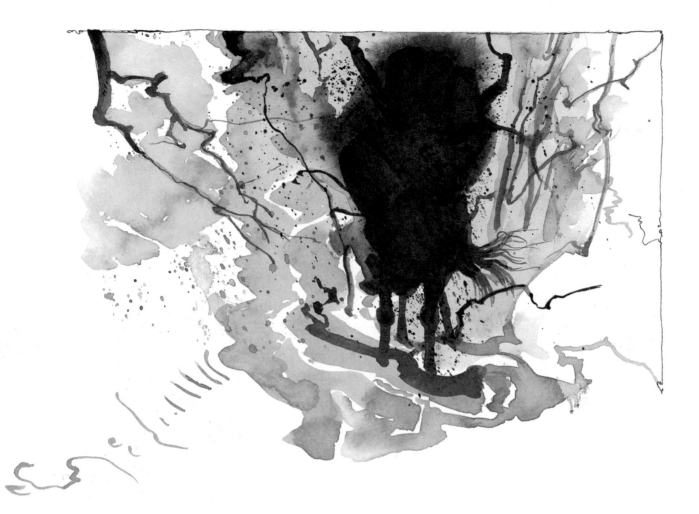

Ichabod gulped. Sweat broke out on his forehead. His breath came short and hard. What should I do? he asked himself silently. What *can* I do? Ichabod knew he couldn't go back the way he came. And he couldn't dash off to the side. Gunpowder would never be able to outrun a ghost or goblin or whatever the creature was. The only chance was forward—across the bridge. Could he make it? Ichabod didn't know. But he knew he'd have to try.

Ichabod decided to stall for time. He'd ask the creature behind him a question, all the while edging Gunpowder closer to the bridge. "Who are you?" the schoolmaster boldly asked, summoning up all his courage. No reply came. Again, Ichabod shouted his question while nudging Gunpowder forward. "Who ARE you, I say?" Again, there was silence. Ichabod started to whistle a tune to himself.

The figure emerged from the shadows and now stood in the middle of the road. In the haze of moonlight, Ichabod still could not see the creature very well. The schoolmaster could just barely make out that he was a horseman of imposing build. The jet-black horse he was riding was equally powerful. But the horseman's face remained hidden in the dark.

Ichabod had no desire to linger and find out who the man was. He kicked Gunpowder's sides, trying to get the horse to move faster. For one of the few times during the return trip, Gunpowder obeyed Ichabod's command and moved slightly faster. But the horseman behind also moved faster, keeping pace. Ichabod's mouth and lips were so dry that he couldn't whistle anymore. From head to heel, he was shaking. Beneath his saddle, the schoolmaster could feel Gunpowder's muscles tightening, too.

Ichabod looked back at his pursuer once more. At that moment, on a slight slope in the road, the figure was set in relief against the sky. Ichabod was thunderstruck. For rising to a chilling height and cloaked completely in black was a horseman without any head! What was even more terrifying was that the horseman's head appeared to be stuck on his saddle!

Horror ripped through every fiber in Ichabod's body. Gripping the reins tightly, he kicked and whipped Gunpowder as hard as he could. The schoolmaster would tolerate no resistance this time. He'd force—even *shove*—the horse across the bridge if he had to. The wincing pain in his flanks told Gunpowder that Ichabod meant business. And the horse responded.

Away the two dashed. Gunpowder was galloping furiously, and Ichabod whipped him to go faster and still faster. But in the same instant that Ichabod and Gunpowder bolted forward, so did the Headless Horseman and his steed. Both riders were at full speed now. Stones flew and sparks flashed as they tore down the road to the bridge ahead. Ichabod's flimsy garments fluttered in the air with every bound. He was so desperate to reach the bridge that his head was almost in front of Gunpowder's. Ichabod could see the breath rushing out of the horse's nose and mouth.

"Come on, Gunpowder!" shouted the schoolmaster. "Faster! FASTER!"

The Headless Horseman was gaining on them. The bridge seemed so close and yet so far. Seconds passed like hours. Could they make it? Or would they be the horseman's latest victims?

"You've got to go *faster*, Gunpowder," pleaded Ichabod. "Just a little farther now. You can do it. Come on! MOVE!"

In a burst of energy, Gunpowder actually went faster. Even though the horseman was getting closer, Gunpowder had somehow picked up speed. Bouncing up and down on the saddle, Ichabod could plainly see the wooden planks of the bridge now.

Once more, Ichabod dug his heels into Gunpowder. But then, suddenly, the straps holding his saddle broke. Ichabod screamed and clasped his arms around Gunpowder's neck. In that split second, the saddle fell off and crashed to the road. Ichabod was now riding bareback!

41

Glancing back over his shoulder, the schoolmaster saw the saddle fall directly into the path of the onrushing horseman. Maybe that will slow him down, hoped Ichabod. But a chill went through him when, without so much as dipping its eyes downward, the horseman's steed easily galloped over the saddle. It never broke stride.

Facing forward again, Ichabod took heart. He was about to cross the bridge! The churchyard was just off to the right.

''Cross that bridge, Gunpowder,'' yelled Ichabod, ''and we're saved!''

But as soon as he said this, Ichabod felt something panting and blowing close behind. Wheeling around, he saw the horseman and his black steed just a few yards back. White, smoky breath steamed from the horse's nostrils. Then, the clattering of hooves on wood made Ichabod turn forward again. He was now on the bridge. Another sharp kick to Gunpowder's flanks carried schoolmaster and horse across and over to the other side. They made it!

Immediately, Ichabod turned around to see if the Headless Horseman would vanish in a flash of fire and brimstone. But just then he saw the horseman rear on his steed. Rising in his stirrups, the Headless Horseman hurled something round straight at Ichabod across the bridge. It was the horseman's head!

With amazing force, it whooshed through the air. Ichabod tried to dodge it. But he was too late. With a splatter, it smashed into the schoolmaster's own head. The blow knocked Ichabod to the ground. He sprawled there, unconscious. Gunpowder, frightened out of his wits, cried out and galloped off. Then the horseman and his black steed flew over the churchyard wall and vanished into thin air among the graves.

The next morning, Gunpowder was found wandering without a saddle through an open field. His eyes were glassy and twitching. And even though the sun was shining brightly, Gunpowder was shivering.

The farmer had laid out breakfast for Ichabod Crane. But the schoolmaster never showed. Nor did he appear for lunch or for supper. And Ichabod did not go to the schoolhouse that morning for class. With no teacher there, the children dismissed themselves early and scooted home.

When the children returned home so early, their parents became worried. What had happened to the schoolmaster? A search party was organized and set off looking for Ichabod. In the middle of the road leading to the bridge by the churchyard, the search party found a saddle covered with dust. There were also two separate sets of horses' hooves that had cut deeply into the road. One set was definitely Gunpowder's. And on the far side of the bridge was Ichabod Crane's small wool hat. Near it were the remains of a shattered pumpkin.

The bridge, brook, churchyard, and surrounding woods were all thoroughly searched. But the body of Ichabod Crane was never found. His mysterious disappearance prompted a great deal of gossip and idle speculation. Some said Ichabod had been carried away by the Headless Horseman. Others said the schoolmaster merely fled in fear for his life, either from the Headless Horseman or from Brom Bones. Still others ventured that Ichabod Crane had left teaching entirely and entered politics in New York City!

No one was really sure what had happened to Ichabod Crane. And no one ever found out. Every time the subject of the shattered pumpkin came up, though, Brom Bones would let out a loud laugh. Some of the villagers suspected Brom knew more about the matter than he let on. After all, they said, Brom did marry Katrina soon after the schoolmaster disappeared.

But it was the old country wives of Sleepy Hollow who had the final word. They insisted that Ichabod Crane had been spirited away by supernatural means. This was the explanation given and accepted most often in the coming years.

Eventually, another schoolmaster was hired. And another schoolhouse was built, though in a different section of the valley. The old schoolhouse, deserted and fallen into decay, had never been disturbed. No one dared. For it was said that the old schoolhouse was haunted. And sometimes, late at night, passersby would swear they heard a sound inside—just like a low whistle.